Magical Beginnings LLC
www.FairyVillageBooks.com

Magical Beginnings LLC 10940 S. Parker Road #971 Parker, CO 80134

ISBN: 9780692593103

This book is dedicated to my two amazing children, Ryan and Logan, who remind me each and every day how amazing and magical life is. For their brilliant minds, and beautiful hearts, they are my inspiration and my role models. I love you both to the moon and back.

"If you want your children to be intelligent, read them fairy tales. If you want them to be more intelligent, read them more fairy tales."

-Albert Einstein

Fairy Village Series

The Tooth Fairy Story

Written By Lisa Gordon

Illustrated By Kate Solenova

Have you ever wondered about the Tooth Fairy? Who is she? Where does she live? Where do the teeth go? And how does she get in and out of your home?

You see, somewhere, in another land, far away, there is a magical place called Fairy Village. A fairy is a magical being whose job is to be a bringer of joy. Each fairy is here to serve a very specific purpose. Each one possesses their own specialty and will become a part of that division inside Fairy Village.

The Music Division

The Music Fairies share their gift with the world through their lovely harmonies. They sculpt and create magnificent wooden instruments that they use to play their beautiful songs. Have you ever felt as though the leaves on the trees or the babbling brook were playing a tune? Have you ever felt sad and then suddenly a song floated into your head that cheered you up? That is your Music Fairy.

The Nature Division

The Nature Fairies have quite a big job indeed. They are responsible for the beautiful landscape you see all around you.

They also protect the animals each and every day. They make sure the sun shines down, helping the plants to grow and keeping the animals nice and warm. Then they make certain the moon rises each night to greet the animals who awake in the evening to frolic and play.

The Holiday Division

The Holiday Fairies have a most joyous job indeed. At Halloween time, they cast a gorgeous glow over the town and make the moon just a little bigger. They paint the leaves a lovely shade of amber in the fall, just in time for Thanksgiving. At Easter, they add extra color and sparkle to the flowers to make the world just a little brighter. And at Christmastime they add sparkle to the snow, berries to the evergreen branches, and a twinkle to all the lights to make the world just a little merrier.

The Watcher Division

The Watcher Fairies have a very essential role. Their job is to watch over the children of the world to protect them and alert the other fairies to their needs. If a child is feeling sad, the Watchers may send a Music Fairy to cheer him up. If they are feeling alone, the Watchers may send a Nature Fairy to surround them with beautiful butterflies. The Watchers use their magical crystal to keep an eye on their kids from Fairy Village, or sometimes they will travel to the Human World to check on them. The animals work alongside the Watchers and report to them anything special they should know.

The Architect Division

Architect Fairies are perhaps one of the most important. I'm going to tell you a secret that no one from the Human World knew up until now... The fairies live in another land all their own to stay safe and protected. This way they can have new magic to bring to us every day. So they must have a way to come into the Human World safely and quietly. That is through a door. Each fairy has their own door they use to come into their family's home. And that door is designed especially for each fairy by the Architects. They work with each fairy to find what she needs, and then they draw up the plans to create the doors.

Have you ever found your fairy's door?

Assignment Board
Child – Fairy:

Ryan – Isabella
Logan – Grace
Barbara – Lucy
Brad – Mary
Laura – Francine
Erin – Seraphina
Paul – Brianna

The Tooth Division

And of course, there are the Tooth Fairies.

Most people believe that there is one Tooth Fairy who flies around the world every night collecting teeth and leaving gifts. Can you imagine one little fairy with all that work to do every night?

Well actually, each and every family has their own Tooth Fairy that is assigned especially to them. This is why some children get coins, some get dollars, and some get other special presents. Each Tooth Fairy leaves her own special gift. And up until now, no one has ever known how they come into the house.

Yes fairies are always around us. We each have our own special fairy to watch over us and help us.

If you stop and pay attention, someday you may notice a beautiful tune in the air, or an unexplained feeling of joy suddenly filling your heart. At times you may just feel a light breeze on your face or through your hair; this is the fairies' wings brushing against you as they fly.

This story is the story of Annabelle; a very special Tooth Fairy during her first night on the job with the very special family she was assigned to.

Annabelle was a young fairy who worked in the Tooth Division. She had eagerly gone through her training at the academy and was thrilled at the idea of being assigned to a new family. She had spent hours mastering the art of pixie dust for flight; countless days crafting her wand that would turn each child's tooth into a special gift for them. She had poured over drawing after drawing with the Architect Fairies to create her door that would become her portal into the Human World and her family's home.

But still Annabelle was a worrier. She wanted to spread joy and magic so eagerly but she worried that she would get it all wrong.

No matter how hard she tried, she could not master turning a tooth into her special coin that would be the gift to her kids. Each day she practiced, and each day she created some interesting gifts... but never any coins.

One day Gwendolyn, the Head Fairy, came to Annabelle with exciting news.

"Your family is almost ready for you, Annabelle!" she proclaimed.

"They are?!" squealed Annabelle.

"Yes my dear, they are. It is a home with two boys and a little girl. Danny, the oldest boy, is about to lose his first tooth any day now. The Watchers tell me he is quite excited about it."

"Any day now!" Annabelle's heart sank a little. How would she ever be ready in time? Would she be the first Tooth Fairy in history to let a child down?

"Annabelle, remember," said Gwendolyn, "you have to feel it in your heart. You have the power inside of you to create anything you want; you just have to believe in yourself".

"Ok", said Annabelle, "I'll try".

L ater that night, Annabelle lay awake in her bed. She knew that anytime now, the bell in her cottage could ring, signaling that it was time to fly. She got out of her bed to practice some more. But the more nervous she felt, the worse it got. With each wave of her wand, her practice teeth turned into one thing worse than the last.

"Sure, what child doesn't dream of waking up with a potato under their pillow?" Annabelle whispered.

She folded her arms and laid her head on them. And finally, she fell asleep.

The next day, Annabelle awoke feeling defeated. She couldn't help but remember how carefree she had felt in the Tooth Academy; the wonderful days when everything felt easy and light. Now that she had to do it for real, she felt as though it were impossible. It came so easy to everyone else. Why not to her? But still, she had a family to care for and she needed to get it right.

Meanwhile, in the Human World, Danny was getting ready for lunch. He had spent the morning playing pirates in his treehouse with his brother, Jason. Their little sister, Mikayla, had insisted on being the ship's captain, so they agreed to let her play. Mom was going to let them have a picnic in their treehouse. They lowered the basket they had tied to a branch with a pulley system.

"Drop the food and step away, argh!" cried Danny.

"Oh my, what ferocious pirates!" teased mom as she placed each lunch bag into the basket. Danny pulled them up and they eagerly grabbed their loot.

"Argh, and what about me strawberries?" Jason probed.

"They be out of strawberries, ye'll have to live with apples" replied mom, in her best piratey voice.

"Thanks Mommy!" Mikayla yelled from the top of the tree house.

The kids laughed and began to eat. Suddenly, Danny heard a strange sound and felt a little "pop". He had taken a bite of his apple, which had been enough to pop out his loose tooth.

"Mom!" he cried. "My tooth, I lost my first tooth!"

Mom grabbed the camera and Danny smiled his new toothless grin. He could not wait to put it under his pillow that night for the Tooth Fairy.

As Annabelle bustled around tooth village, she suddenly stopped. She had a feeling of joy and excitement in her stomach but she wasn't quite sure why. Something had happened and she could not help but smile. "That's your fairy instincts you know", said Katrina, Annabelle's friend.

"What are you talking about?" Annabelle asked.

"That smile, that feeling in your gut. You're connecting with your family, with your kids. The magic is inside of you Annabelle. You can do it. You just have to believe in yourself".

No sooner had Annabelle returned to her cottage than the bell began to ring.

"It's time!" she exclaimed.

She sat down and began to write her note. When she was done, she quickly tucked it into her satchel along with a handful of pixie dust, grabbed her wand and took a deep breath. She had to get it right; she had to believe she could.

Annabelle made her way through the village and with one last look back, trudged forward into the enchanted woods. She entered the clearing where she saw thousands of beautiful trees in front of her. Each one had the name of the family each fairy was assigned to. She felt lost. Though stunningly beautiful, the forest was so big and wide, how would she ever know which tree was her door, her portal to get to Danny's house?

Shea

Anderson

She closed her eyes and let her heart fill with joy. She pictured Danny smiling in the morning and how happy he would feel. When she opened her eyes, in the distance, a tree began to glow. She walked towards it, and lo and behold, the tree's inscription read "Parker", Danny's family name. She sprinkled her dust and pressed her hand gently against the tree's trunk. Sure enough, a door knob appeared. She turned the knob and when next she knew, she was inside Danny's house.

anny's house was dark and quiet. She silently closed the door behind her and was delighted to see that the Architects had followed all her wishes. It looked beautiful! She looked once more at her notes. The Watchers had said Danny's room was down the hallway, first bedroom on the left. She took a deep breath and flew to the room to find a young boy, tucked sweetly in his bed, fast asleep.

Ever so softly, she reached under his pillow and pulled out a tooth. She felt delighted but also so afraid. What if she couldn't do it? She gently placed her note by Danny's bedside. The pixie dust on the note glimmered in the moonlight. Annabelle gently set the tooth beside it.

She closed her eyes and heard Gwendolyn's words in her head. "You have the power inside of you to create anything you want; you just have to believe in yourself".

"I believe in myself", she whispered.   And with a wave of her hand, she felt the joy rush through her heart and into her wand. Beautiful pixie dust burst through and when she opened her eyes she no longer saw a tooth, but a beautiful coin. She had done it! Annabelle had never been more proud of herself. She blew Danny a kiss and quietly, quickly slipped out of his room and back through her door to Fairy Village.

In the morning when Danny awoke, he immediately thought of his tooth. He ran his hand under his pillow. It was gone! When he sat up, he saw something shimmer in the sunlight by his nightstand. He pulled on his glasses and looked. There was a beautiful golden coin unlike any he had ever seen before. And next to it: a note. It read:

You lost your first tooth, hooray!
I am your personal tooth fairy and I have been so excited to come and see you! Have you ever seen my secret door? All of us fairies have one to come and check on our kids. *Giggle
Love Your friend,
The Tooth Fairy

Danny was so excited he could hardly stand it. He couldn't wait

to run downstairs to show his mom and brother and sister. But for a moment, he closed his eyes, took a deep breath, and smiled.

And somewhere, in another land far away, so did Annabelle..

CPSIA information can be obtained at www.ICGtesting.com
Printed in the USA
LVIW01n2300260716
497928LV00013B/31